The Peddler's Gift

Maxine Rose Schur

pictures by

Kimberly Bulcken Root

New York · Dial Books for Young Readers

Published by Dial Books for Young Readers
A division of Penguin Putnam Inc.
345 Hudson Street
New York, New York 10014

Text copyright ©1985, 1999 by Maxine Rose Schur
Pictures copyright ©1999 by Kimberly Bulcken Root
All rights reserved
Originally published in different form
as *Shnook the Peddler* by Dillon Press, Inc.

Designed by Julie Rauer
Printed in Hong Kong on acid-free paper
First Edition
1 3 5 7 9 10 8 6 4 2

Library of Congress Cataloging in Publication Data
Schur, Maxine.
[Shnook the peddler]
The peddler's gift / Maxine Rose Schur;
pictures by Kimberly Bulcken Root.—1st ed.
p. cm.
Summary: A young boy in turn-of-the-century rural Russia learns
that appearances are often deceiving after he steals a dreidel
from the traveling peddler Shnook.
ISBN 0-8037-1978-7
[1. Peddlers and peddling—Fiction. 2. Jews—Russia—Fiction.]
I. Root, Kimberly Bulcken, ill. II. Title.
PZ7.S3964Pe 1999 [Fic]—dc21 98-36171 CIP AC

The illustrations were created with watercolor and pencil.

For Aaron

M.R.S.

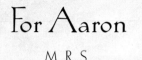

For Samuel

K.B.R.

In Korovenko, late summer was hot and damp. The rye grew high as corn, the air smelled of fallen plums, and near our thatched-roof hut the river babbled all day like a happy baby.

But in all this warm beauty there was little time for play. From sunrise to sunset we boys studied Torah, and after that it was supper, prayers, and bed. On Shabbos we rested and strolled through the plum orchards at the edge of the village. Only on Wednesday, when our school let out early, did we get a chance to run, yell, play Cossacks, and swish our bare feet in the tickle-cold waters of the river.

One Wednesday afternoon my friend Moshe and I were making swords from fallen oak branches, when he asked, "Leibush, have you seen Shnook?"

"What?" I cried. "Is Shnook here?"

"Sure. He arrived from Pinsk last night and slept in the synagogue. Yankel saw his wagon there this morning."

"Maybe he'll come to our house again!" I yelled, jumping up. "Maybe he's there now!" Grabbing my sword, I ran up the riverbank toward home. Every peddler who happened through our village brought merriment, but Shnook brought more laughs than any of them.

Lucky me. There at the side of our hut was his broken-down cart. I opened the door and saw my father and the peddler sitting at our table, drinking glasses of tea. Standing between them, my mother cut two large slices of her honey cake. The peddler chewed the cake slowly. His face was thin and dry, and his hands were bony and rough from driving his wagon. His smile was warm, yet he spoke so little, my father once said his words must be weighed, not counted. Shimon was the peddler's real name, but because he seemed a simpleton, the children of Korovenko called him Shnook.

Now Shnook stood up and in his meek voice said, "Please come and see what I have." As I edged closer, he glanced at me, then smiled at my father. "Your boy has grown taller," he said.

"Yes." Papa beamed. "In summer Leibush shoots up like a wildflower."

Shnook smiled at me for several moments, and despite my feeling that he must be a noodle-head, I smiled back.

Some of the older boys said Shnook was not just simple, but bad. They believed he had been put under a spell by the Evil Eye, and that's why he bungled things. Yankel even said Shnook had magic powers and could use certain words to trick you, make you forget your name, cause feathers to sprout from your ears and little stewing onions to grow between your toes. I didn't know what to believe. Papa had many times warned me against gossip. He told me what I didn't see with my eyes not to make up with my mouth. And yet surely this peddler from Pinsk was cut from a different cloth than the other peddlers who traveled through our village.

Other peddlers opened their great bags with a flourish, waved their arms, and smiled like fathers at a wedding as they described their wares in long flowery words.

"Good Jewish wife," they would exclaim, "allow me please to show you the most excellent of stew pots! Here I have, just for your inspection, direct from the fiery kilns of St. Petersburg, a silver-toned tin pot fit for a fat goose at the banquet of the czar, may a thunderbolt strike his head!"

After noisy bargaining, other peddlers would stay for a glass of tea, and then another, a cookie, a slice of honey cake, and more often than not, a supper of soup and groats.

And when the oil lamps were lit, these peddlers who drove from Moscow to Minsk wove tales of intrigue about the czar's court. The whole world lay on their tongues. They brought news from Kiev and Vladivostok. They described the fashions of the cities to the merriment of the women, all the while pinching the cheeks of the youngest children and slipping cinnamon candies into their small hands.

But Shnook was different.

The villagers said that if Shnook sold coffins, people would stop dying. The truth was, nothing he did turned out right. One time he left his goods in Pinsk and traveled to Rovno with an empty bag. Another time he left his bag open near a kitchen door where a goat was tied up. The goat ate five pairs of socks and a hat. Still another time he sold all his wares to himself, then gave them to a poor family.

There's a saying: "When a foolish buyer goes to market, the sellers rejoice." But in Korovenko when Shnook the Peddler arrived, the buyers rejoiced! If someone actually expressed interest in his goods, he might exclaim, "Nu? You really want to buy these handkerchiefs? The cloth is thin and the stitching poor. It's better you keep your money."

Worse yet, Shnook had no idea how to buy goods from the wholesalers. He would often end up with such odd things, even he did not know what they were. Once he mistakenly sold shoehorns as spatulas, and another time he bought three-hundred fountain pens—all of them leaking. Shnook has such bad luck, people joked, even his fountain pens cry!

Now, as we all watched, he opened his ragged leather bag. He took his goods out so silently, you would have thought he was hiding them rather than presenting them for sale. He carefully laid out red silk ribbons, boxes of matches, small glass bottles of rosewater, great flag-sized squares of cloth, embroidered pillowcases, painted wooden spoons, writing paper and jars of black ink, bone and wood buttons, paper-wrapped packages of needles, brass buttonhooks, pure white cakes of soap nesting in blue tissue, and lace tablecloths all the way from Hungary.

When he came to the religious items, he showed special care. On the table he gently placed Shabbos bread covers, prayer shawls, Shabbos candles, and my favorite, the four-sided Hanukkah tops we called dreidels. Shnook's dreidels were big. They were fist-sized, hand-carved from birch wood, and could spin nearly three minutes without falling!

We gazed wide-eyed at all the glorious new things that transformed our soot-stained hut into a colorful bazaar. Even Papa, who took little notice of such things, looked amazed.

The peddler stood back and stared down at his boots as if discovering two old friends. He always seemed shy when showing his goods, so waited for my mother to make the first move.

My mother, never wishing to cause him discomfort, began to look over the goods, touching many of the items gently, thinking to herself about each one. I watched while she stroked the heavy cotton fabric from Zhitomir. It was deep blue, the color of cornflowers, and I knew my mother would have dearly loved to buy it—to sew it, to dress me up like a scholar. But we were not for that sort of thing. My trousers were made from my father's old ones. My shirt was cut from Mama's discarded dress. Even my jacket had lived a former life as Uncle Solly's coat.

Mama never had more to spend than one ruble, and this time she chose matches, writing paper, and the Shabbos candles. When she had selected her purchases, she asked how much they cost, and the magic was that the peddler always said, "One ruble."

Mama sighed and handed Shnook the ruble. It was then, while he was writing out the receipt, I noticed one of the dreidels under the chair. As he gathered his wares, he did not see the fallen dreidel. I should have picked it up for him, but something inside me froze. I stood in front of the chair, reasoning frantically. He won't miss it; after all, he never notices anything. Besides, I'll just borrow it, and the next time he comes to town, I'll find a way to slip it back to him.

Just then my father's voice interrupted my thoughts. "Shimon, the sky is dark now, and the air is heavy. We would be honored if you would share our supper with us and stay the night."

As always, Shnook made an excuse to go. "Thank you, but Pinsk is still two days away, and I want to get there by Shabbos."

"But, Shimon," my mother asked, "where will you go if it rains?"

The peddler opened the door. "There is my shelter," he said. "My carpet is the road; my ceiling, the sky; and my lamps, the stars."

That night after prayers, I climbed onto my bed above the warm brick oven and listened to the crashing sound of the late summer storm. I had hidden the dreidel under my feather bed, and now I took it out to feel its smooth wood in the dark. My parents had fallen asleep quickly, but I could not sleep. They say a thief has an easy job but difficult dreams. My mind spun like a dreidel as I imagined being in jail, laughed at and scorned. "There is Leibush, the thief, the thief, the thief." I saw my father, my mother, the rabbi, all the villagers pointing at me while the dreidel burned in my hand. Outside, the rain pounded down as if it were crying for me, while nightmarish images stormed through my head. Then suddenly I saw the trusting face of the peddler and realized with a terrible certainty that I had done wrong.

In the dark I laced up my boots and put on my coat. Tucking the dreidel into the pocket, I slipped out into the rain.

I ran through the village, heading for the synagogue, for I hoped if Shnook would be in any dry place tonight, he would be there. The night was wild. In the black sky, ghostly clouds traveled quickly across the heavens. The wind howled like a dog in pain, and the rain beat down so angrily that the twisted cobblestone streets were changed into rivers.

Lights were on in the synagogue. I peeked through the side window but it streamed with rain, and I could see only someone's shadow. I went to the door and found it slightly open. I had straight in my mind what I was going to say to him. I would confess my sin right away and give back the dreidel. Then I would ask him to forgive me. I trembled as I entered the synagogue, partly from the cold but mostly from fear. An oil lamp burned brightly. I walked in, the rain dripping off me, forming small puddles on the floor. Suddenly I heard singing in a voice so strong and beautiful, I couldn't move. The peddler was not here! Someone else, some powerful-voiced traveler had sought shelter in the synagogue tonight. My disappointment was so great, I began to cry.

The man broke off his splendid song and walked toward me. His face was bright with such happiness that at first I did not recognize him.

"Leibush!" he said. "What are you doing here on this terrible night?"

His words startled me. For a few horrible seconds I had forgotten why I was there and could do nothing but cry. At last my tears stopped, and I said through chattering teeth, "I came to bring you this. You left it in our home." I handed him the dreidel. "I mean...I stole it." Shnook pulled a handkerchief from his pocket and wiped my face.

"Come," he beckoned, getting dry clothes from his valise. "Change your clothes."

After I had changed, the storm was still raging, so Shnook insisted I remain in the synagogue until it passed. He wrapped himself in his coat and made me sleep on his feather quilt. As we bedded down, I said, "I'm sorry I took your dreidel."

"I know you are," was all he replied.

"But why aren't you angry with me?" I asked.

He looked at me for a few seconds, smoothing his beard. "First of all," he said with a small smile, "I knew you had taken it."

"You knew!"

"I saw you put it in your pocket. Thank the Lord, you are not a good thief!"

"You knew . . . and still you're not angry! Why aren't you angry?" For some reason my own voice had anger in it.

"We are in the Lord's house. There is too much peace here to be angry. You were angry at yourself. That is what really mattered."

The peddler pulled the coat tighter around him. It was too short to cover his feet, and I saw his worn socks dotted with holes.

When we woke, it was still dark. After dressing and praying, he hitched Fresser to his cart and said good-bye. In that gray, dead world that exists before dawn, I watched the peddler steer his old cart down the mud-washed road toward Pinsk.

I turned homeward. My sleeping village lay cold and wet around me, giving off the odor of damp wood and musty hay. I reached home before my parents woke, and climbed back into bed.

Though he returned to Korovenko for many years, I never again called him Shnook. He was Shimon, the Peddler from Pinsk. Shimon the wise, the strong, the kind. The one who left cotton the color of cornflowers by our door, and on Hanukkah a big, birch-carved dreidel.

I have it to this day.

On snowy Hanukkah nights, when the candles burn short and the dreidel spins its lone path across the landscape of our floor, I see him traveling to Pinsk. His carpet, the road; his ceiling, the sky; and his lamps, the stars.